Dip Into A Story

Volume 2

Dip Into A Story

Volume 2

Large Print Edition

Cathy Emma Laybourn

Contents

These stories are also published in
the ebook:

Coffee-break Stories and Tea-time Tales
2nd Collection:
Twenty Magazine Short Stories

The stories were originally published in
various magazines:
Take a Break
Take a Break Fiction Feast
That's Life (Australia)
My Weekly
The Weekly News

Tell Me You Love Me

'So where are you going for your wedding anniversary?' asked Jade during their tea-break.

'The garden centre,' said Yvonne, between clenched teeth.

'The garden centre?'

'Dave's promised me a nice shrub or two.' Seeing the incredulity in her young colleague's face, Yvonne added defensively, 'After all, it's not a big anniversary. It's only twenty-four years.'

Jade's eyes widened. She was just nineteen.

'Sounds pretty big to me!' she said, and then, as her phone beeped, broke off to check it.

'Aaah! It's a text from Finn. He says he loves me lots and sends a bucketload of kisses.'

'That's sweet. How long have you been going out together?' asked Yvonne.

'Ooh, ages. Five months,' said Jade.

Yvonne bit back the caustic comment that sprang to her lips, merely commenting, 'Lovely. Ah well, back to work.'

She had no right to spoil love's young dream, just because Dave hadn't told her he loved her in the last twenty years. The only bucketload of anything that Dave was likely to give her was of concrete for the patio...

Yvonne sighed as she sat down at her till. Dave was fond of her, sure. Although they'd had their ups and downs through the years, she was pretty certain there had never been anyone else.

The trouble was, he never said it. At least, never since that rather drunken party all of fifteen years ago. As they had walked home, he'd stopped dead in the middle of the road and burst out, 'I do love you, Yvonne!'

She'd been waiting ever since for him to say it again. And he never had.

Dave was a man of deeds, not words, she told herself. He worked in the building trade and was never happier than when messing around with a cement mixer. She'd known right from the start that he wasn't the type for flowery romantic gestures.

All the same. It would have been nice if just now and then, he could make the effort...

Gritting her teeth, Yvonne put the next basket-load through the till: a bottle of sparkling wine, a box of chocolates and a birthday card covered in hearts.

She smiled politely at the elderly customer as he rummaged in his wallet. If he could manage romantic gestures at his age, why couldn't Dave?

Her shift seemed to be full of loved-up couples, holding hands, kissing in the queue... Yvonne's cheeks were soon aching from keeping that polite smile on her face.

To rub salt in the wound, the in-store radio was playing nothing but love songs. What would our song be? she wondered. Bob the Builder?

At that point Yvonne came to a decision. Before this anniversary was over, she would get Dave to declare his love for her. She didn't yet know how she'd do it – but there had to be a way.

So after work she did a little extra shopping.

That evening she cooked him his favourite meal: steak with pepper sauce, followed by a chocolate pudding.

She patched his dreadful old work overalls without complaint, and admired his progress with their new patio even though it looked like a bomb site.

Then she snuggled on the sofa with him to watch the footie instead of her usual TV drama, and remembered to cheer whenever he did.

By the evening's end she was bored stiff, although Dave was perfectly happy. But he didn't say he loved her.

For her next attempt, Yvonne changed tack. Tight jeans, that low-cut top that Dave admired, high heels, more make-up than she'd worn all year.

She could still carry it off, she decided, surveying herself in the mirror. Now to take Dave to the pub and ply him with drink.

'Great!' said Dave. 'But why?'

'To celebrate our anniversary tomorrow.' She fluttered her mascaraed eyelashes at him seductively.

'Good idea! That means we won't need to go out again for a special meal.'

Yvonne sighed, and then smiled. There would be no arguments this evening. She just wanted to make Dave happy.

Certainly, at the pub Dave seemed to enjoy himself, especially when she told him she was buying all the drinks. He even commented appreciatively on her provocative wiggle as she walked up to the bar.

But that wasn't the same as telling her he loved her. And although he was very willing for her to play the sexy siren later on, he never said those three little magic words.

Yvonne did her best to prompt him.
'I love you,' she murmured huskily; and it was true. Such a little thing to say, and yet it meant so much. She held her breath and waited for his answer.

'Oh, good.'

In the cool light of day, Yvonne considered her next step.

She could just ask Dave to say it. It was their anniversary, after all... but she had her pride. She didn't want to sound like a needy teenager, demanding demonstrations of love every five minutes.

'Once every five years would be a bonus,' muttered Yvonne, as she began to dig the hole for the new shrubs Dave had bought her. They'd been to the garden centre that morning, and had chosen a pair of hebes: very nice, and not at all romantic.

Dave seemed intent on spending their special day concreting the garden path. Apart from a 'Happy Anniversary' with her morning cup of tea, that had been it.

Yvonne slammed the spade viciously into the soil. Why couldn't he say it, just once? Why was it so hard? What was wrong with her, that he couldn't say it? What was wrong with **him**?

He'll never say it, she thought. Never in a hundred years! And she stamped furiously on the spade.

It gave way beneath her foot. The rusted shaft snapped. Yvonne tumbled over it, shouting 'Ow! Ow! OW!'

Later on, she had to admit that Dave was pretty good. He didn't moan at all about the blood in the car, or the long wait in hospital for stitches and a tetanus injection; or the fact that as soon as they got back home, Yvonne burst into tears.

'It's nothing,' she said, sniffling in the car, 'just delayed shock, I expect.'

He hugged her. But still he didn't say it.

It doesn't matter, thought Yvonne. Hasn't he just shown he loves me? That's enough – that should see me through another year.

So she wiped her tears away determinedly as she opened the car door and limped up the path.

'No, stop!' cried Dave suddenly. 'Stop there!
Don't look down! Close your eyes! Oh,
heck – I totally forgot!'

'Forgot what?'

'I should have smoothed it over,' he said
wretchedly. 'And now the concrete's set
while we were out! In all the rush, I didn't
think about it.'

Yvonne looked down. She saw a giant heart
drawn on the path, and written inside it:

D LOVES Y.

'Sorry,' said Dave, blushing fiery red. 'It's
just habit. I always do it when I lay a
concrete floor.'

She found her voice. 'You always do it?'

He nodded, wincing. 'It's in any number of houses, hidden under the flooring. I know it's a really stupid thing to do. I mean, I'm not a teenager! But I'll put another skim over it first thing tomorrow, I promise.'

'No rush,' said Yvonne, gazing at the enormous heart in the middle of the path. 'I can live with it for now.'

'But it's there for everyone to see!'

'It is, isn't it?' mused Yvonne. 'Set in stone. It could last there for a hundred years or more...' She grinned, and then reached up to kiss Dave's burning cheek.

'Tell you what,' she said. 'I'll let you cover it over – in a little while. Maybe for our silver wedding anniversary!'

One Hundred Lines

At first I blamed the children.

Well, you would, wouldn't you? It was only natural. It was my first term at the primary school as a teaching assistant, and I didn't yet know the children well.

They were a friendly, lively lot; but a bit too lively, in some cases. So of course they were the first ones I thought of when I saw the lines. After all, who else could have done it? Any child could easily slip into the stationery cupboard. It was never locked.

It wasn't so much a cupboard as a tiny, chilly room. It was never warm in there. Its shelves were heaped with exercise books, boxes of pencils and stacks of paper – all the paraphernalia of a busy school. Part of my job was to keep it tidy and order new stock.

On this particular morning, I was counting out new exercise books when I noticed one had some writing in it.

'Now, who's done that?' I muttered, opening it up to look.

I must not shout.
I must not shout.
I must not shout...

The same line was repeated in wobbly pencil all down the page.

'Well!' I said. 'What will they get up to next?' And at break-time I took the book along to the staffroom.

'You don't make children write lines as a punishment, do you?' I asked the teachers as they sipped their tea.

'Not any more,' said Mrs O'Neill, the Head.

'Twenty years ago we did, but not these days.'

'That's what I thought.' I showed the teachers the book. 'It must be somebody's idea of a joke. Does anyone recognise the handwriting?' The teachers peered and tutted and shook their heads.

'Probably disguised,' said Mrs O'Neill. 'I wouldn't put it past Ryan or Jasmin in Year Six. I'll have a little word.'

So she had a little word, but reported back to me that nobody had owned up.

'All wide-eyed and innocent,' she said. 'I don't think it's worth making a big fuss over, but let me know if it happens again.'

It was a week later that I went to fetch a dozen new maths books from the cupboard. I reached for the pile.

There, in the topmost book, was the same childish handwriting, sprawling across the page:

I must sit quietly.
I must sit quietly.
I must sit quietly.

I frowned. If it was Ryan or Jasmin writing this, I would have expected a bit more imagination. 'I must not put worms in the washbasin and tell the infants they're practising swimming for the Worm Olympics;' that was more Ryan's style.

When I showed the book to Mrs O'Neill, she sighed.

'Silly children! Have you noticed anyone lurking around the stationery cupboard lately?'

'Nobody.'

'Well, I'm not happy,' said Mrs O'Neill.
And in the next school assembly, she had
another word, not such a little one this time.

'That should sort the problem out,' she said.

It seemed to, for a while. Until I opened a
new batch of shrink-wrapped yellow-covered
books, and the top one fell open in my hands.

There was page after page of it. The same
uneven handwriting, inexpertly joined up.
There must have been a hundred lines, or
more:

I must be good.
I must be good.
I must be good... on and on.

I stood and stared, totally flummoxed,
because these books had been tightly
wrapped in plastic. The children couldn't
possibly have got at them.

Suddenly it felt ice-cold in that tiny space, and as constricted as a prison. The walls seemed to close in on me, and I felt my heart start to pound. Pulling myself together, I hurried out.

But when I explained this new conundrum to Mrs O'Neill, to my surprise she laughed.

'Well, that's a relief!' she said. 'It means it's not our pupils after all – it's a problem at the suppliers. They've probably got someone working in the packing department who thinks it's funny. Give them a ring.'

So I did. The suppliers denied all knowledge – but then, as Mrs O'Neill said, they would, wouldn't they?

Anyway, after that I took to checking the new books as soon as they were delivered. There were no lines to be seen, and I decided Mrs O'Neill had been right.

Until the day I did a full stock-take.

Unwrapping a batch of English books, I flipped through them, and then stacked them in piles. As I turned to the maths books, I heard a pile slither to the ground behind me.

'Botheration!' I stooped to pick them up. The one at the bottom of the pile was lying open, upside down. I turned it over – and I froze. I'd just checked all these books. They had been blank. So how could this one now be full of lines?

I must not talk.
I must not talk.
I must not talk...

I jumped at a sound behind me. The maths books were slowly sliding off the shelf – and as they tumbled through the air I could glimpse the ill-formed letters on the flapping pages.

I must not talk...

I shot out of that stationery cupboard like a cat on roller skates. Out in the corridor, I leaned against the door, my heart thumping, taking big gasps of air.

It took me a good five minutes to pluck up the courage to go back in. When I did, everything was still. I tidied up the books with shaking hands. The ones with lines I hid beneath the bottom shelf; and then I got out of there fast.

This time, I said nothing to Mrs O'Neill. She'd never believe me – or she might suspect me of writing the lines myself! Either way, she'd think I was going round the bend.

Maybe I was. All day, I was distracted. Could I have missed those handwritten lines the first time round? I didn't think so.

The trouble was, I could only think of one alternative solution, and I didn't care for it at all. I'd never had much time for ghost stories...

At half past three, when the children had gone home, I sought out Mrs O'Neill in her office. I had some questions for her.

I started by discussing the stock-take and the orders. Normal stuff. Then, trying to be casual, I asked, 'You know the stationery cupboard – has it ever been used for anything else? It's more like a little room.'

'It **is** a little room. When I started working here, it used to be the headmaster's office,' Mrs O'Neill recalled. 'And a poky little cubbyhole it was too.'

'An office? You'd hardly fit a desk in there!'

'It was certainly a tight squeeze!' she agreed.

'The Head back then didn't use it much, although sometimes he'd make children work in there on their own if they'd been disruptive. Later on they built this extension and moved the office.'

'I see. Um…' I couldn't think of any casual way of asking my next question. 'Has any child ever died while they've been at the school?'

'My goodness! Certainly not since I've worked here, and that's over thirty years,' she said, startled.

'What about before that?'

'Well, the school was built in 1963, so I suppose it's possible, but I'm not aware of any deaths. Why ever do you ask?'

'Just something somebody told me,' I said vaguely. 'Who was the Head back then?'

'John Garnett. He was still Head when I arrived here as a newly qualified teacher, but he retired soon afterwards. He died, oh, twenty years ago.'

'What was he like?'

'Well, he was strict. The old-fashioned sort of headmaster, you know? He didn't stand for any nonsense.' Mrs O'Neill studied me with concern. 'You're looking very pale, Jan! Are you all right?'

'Just a headache.'

'You should go home now,' she said gently.

'I will.' Despite her kindness, I dared not tell her about the lines. But now they were imprinted on my mind. **I must be good...
I must not talk...** Where had they come from? What had happened in that little, chilly room?

That question haunted me all evening and broke into my sleep. I had a restless night.

Next morning, heavy-eyed, I forced myself out of bed, resolved to find the answer. While I'd been lying awake, an idea had come to me.

I approached Mrs O'Neill again.

'You know you said the school was built in 1963? That means its sixtieth anniversary is coming up. I thought it might be nice to research its history. Are any of the old school records still around?'

She was delighted. 'What a good idea! Year Six could do a project on it. It would be excellent for their writing skills! And I'm sure there's a whole heap of old books somewhere...' Even as she spoke, she was starting to rummage in a cupboard.

And before I knew it, I was in the Year Six classroom with a pile of school registers, ledgers and photographs, surrounded by a crowd of children looking through them and giggling at the funny clothes that people wore back then.

There was a series of black and white photos from 1963 that showed each class of children lined up in front of the new school.

In the middle of every group stood a tall, gaunt, sternly frowning man. Mr Garnett. He looked like the sort who would make them toe the line, all right...

'Look at this!' said Ryan indignantly. 'They used to wallop the kids back in the 1960's!'

He'd found a punishment book. He began to read out the list of children who'd been given lines, detentions, and the strap.

'I'm glad they don't do that any more!' he exclaimed.

'So am I,' I agreed, as I glanced down the list. One name immediately sprang out at me. It appeared again and again: Gary Ferriman.

He was always in trouble: shouting at a dinner lady, fighting, destroying the nature table... He got the strap a lot in 1964; although after September, he got given lines to write instead. More lines than all the other children put together.

The punishments were recorded in a neat, slanting copperplate. **Fifty lines in the headmaster's office. Sixty lines. One hundred lines...**

But in December his punishments abruptly stopped. In 1965, he wasn't mentioned.

So had he reformed?

I turned to the old class registers. Here was Gary again: his address was 8 Harville Row. But after 1965 there was just a long, black pencil line drawn through his name.

He must have moved away. That was the rational answer. There was nothing except my imagination to connect him with the lines in the cupboard.

So why, when I studied the class photos, did I immediately notice the thin, scruffy boy staring out from one of them? Why did his sad face seem to implore me?

And how did I know, even before I checked the listing on the back, what his name would be? Gary Ferriman...

I took a different route home that day, down Harville Row. It was a building site: a noticeboard informed me that a development of new homes was going up.

Number 8 was a pile of rubble with a yellow digger burrowing in the garden.   There was no-one here to ask what had happened to Gary. Nothing else I could do.

But a few days later, as I fetched a pile of books from the stationery cupboard, I saw the writing again:

I must not laugh.
I must not laugh.
I must not laugh.

This time I did not rush out in a panic.
I felt pity for the boy shut in that tiny, cold, cramped room, writing out his hundred lines. And I thought of Mr Garnett with dislike.

That morning, in assembly, Mrs O'Neill announced, 'We have a surprise visitor here today! I'd like to welcome Mrs Lang, who was one of the very first teachers at our school, back in the nineteen-sixties.

She's come to talk to Year Six about those days.'

Irene Lang was a quiet, grey-haired lady in her late eighties, but she was a big hit with the children, with plenty of anecdotes to tell.

I stood at the back of the Year Six classroom, listening in. She didn't mention punishments, however, and when Ryan asked about the strap, she deftly steered the subject away.

Afterwards, I took her to the staffroom for a cup of tea.

'The children really enjoyed your talk,' I said. 'But there's one thing I'd like to ask you. It's about a boy called Gary Ferriman, who was at the school back in 1963. I couldn't help noticing his name in the old punishment book; it appeared so many times.'

I didn't expect her to remember one boy from so long ago, but she immediately responded.

'Gary! My goodness, yes. What a difficult child he was! He'd fight, he'd lash out, kick and shout. He'd end up going to Mr Garnett's office nearly every day.'

'And Mr Garnett made him write lines?'

She nodded. 'He shut Gary in his little office on his own. I daresay it wouldn't be allowed now... but it was the only thing that seemed to work.'

'What happened to Gary?'

She sighed. 'One day Mr Garnett had a big row with him. I heard shouting in the office. Then it all went quiet – I could just hear Gary crying...'

She bit her lip. 'Gary stayed in that office for the rest of the day. Once the children had gone home, Mr Garnett came to see me. I remember how his face looked: grey and drawn... and he told me he had done a terrible thing.'

I gripped my hands tightly together. I did not want to know; but I had to ask. 'What had happened?'

'Mr Garnett had lost his temper with Gary. He'd shouted that he was a waste of space, nothing but trouble, that he needed teaching a lesson.'

I was filled with dread. 'And then?'

'Then Gary had broken down in tears. It all came out: what his life was like at home. He had a stepfather who got drunk every day and beat him. Gary wasn't allowed to play or talk or make any noise at all.

He had to sit still and silent or he'd get beaten even worse. His mother was too terrified to stand up for him.'

'The poor boy!'

'Exactly. No wonder he kept getting into trouble, Mr Garnett said: all his anger and unhappiness came out at school. But you know what?' Mrs Lang gave me a sad half-smile. 'Gary said he liked school best when he got punished. Isn't that strange?'

'How sad. I suppose it was still better than home.'

'It must have been. Gary liked sitting in the Headmaster's little office, he said, and writing lines. He felt safe in there. After that, the Head let Gary work in there whenever he wanted – which was most days.'

'So that explains all the entries in the punishment book,' I said.

She nodded. 'Gary asked him to put it in the book as lines so the other children wouldn't realise. He had a soft heart, did Mr Garnett.'

I thought of the stern, gaunt man in the photograph, whom I had wronged.
'Why did Gary leave the school?' I asked.

'Oh, the family moved away. Mr Garnett called the stepfather in, and told him he would have to change his behaviour. He notified the social workers too, but before they got round to doing anything, the family upped and left. They'd done a runner without paying their rent.'

'Do you know where they went to?'

She shook her head. 'We never found out.'

When Irene had departed, I walked into the stationery cupboard, where Gary had felt safe.

I must not laugh. I must not talk. Not the teacher's commands, but his stepfather's...

So why did the lines keep appearing here? What was Gary trying to tell me?

'What is it, Gary?' I whispered.

There was the thin rustle of paper behind me. I turned and saw the book, with its childish, pencilled scrawl.

I must not hide in the shed.
I must not hide in the shed...

I stared at the page, and felt a chill creep over me again...

That day I went home past Harville Row, and stopped at number 8.

The digger had gone: the place was deserted. A pile of bricks showed where Gary's house had been. I wriggled through a gap in the temporary fencing and picked my way across the rubble.

This forlorn patch must have been Gary's back garden. And that heap of planks, I guessed, had once been the shed. When the digger tore it down, it had left behind a litter of broken, rusty tools: a bit of spade, a scatter of nails, splinters of wood everywhere... and peeping out between them, something yellowish-white.

I bent down to look, clearing the soil away. It was a bone. And as I frantically dug around it, I realised the full, pitiable truth of Gary's fate.

'It's extraordinary!' exclaimed Mrs O'Neill. 'To think one of our children could have been murdered, all those years ago!'

The teachers in the staffroom murmured sombre, horrified agreement.

'If the police hadn't received that anonymous phone call, the diggers might have ploughed straight through his grave and never known.'

'Have they traced whoever made the call?' somebody asked.

Mrs O'Neill shook her head. 'It was from a phone box. Probably some youth who shouldn't have been trespassing on the site… but it's just as well they did!'

Quietly, I left the staffroom.

I went into the stationery cupboard and closed the door. The confined space was as still and cold as ever. I picked up the book I had left on the shelf, with its childish lines of writing.

I must not hide in the shed.

Then I picked up a pencil, and underneath the lines I wrote:

You need not hide any more, Gary.
You may play. You may laugh.
You are safe now.
You are safe for ever.

And I knew that somehow, somewhere, he would understand.

The Call of the Chocolate Biscuit

Craig peered into the cupboard with a frown. 'Where are those nice chocolate biscuits?'

'Um...' said Robyn guiltily.

Her husband turned and stared at her. 'What? In your stomach? **All** of them?'

'That's the trouble with working from home,' sighed Robyn. 'Too much temptation.'

'Yes, I can tell!' said Craig, patting her midriff.

'Do you think I'm putting on weight?' said Robyn anxiously.

He rolled his eyes. 'If you eat a whole packet of chocolate biscuits at once, what do you expect?'

'It wasn't a full packet,' she argued. 'And they're so nice!'

'They're bad for you,' said Craig severely. 'If the temptation's that great, then keep them out of reach.'

Ruefully, Robyn thought that her waistband did feel a little tight. 'I will,' she promised.

So next time she bought a packet of her favourite biscuits, she put them right at the back of a drawer. Sitting at her desk, she tried to concentrate on her work.

But she could hear those chocolate biscuits calling. Just one with her coffee; that was all she needed... Only one.

By lunchtime she was staring at an empty packet.

'How did **that** happen?' she wailed.

She walked down to the shop that evening to buy another pack. It was quite a trek without the car – but she didn't want Craig to guess her weakness, so she told him she was just going for a walk.

Next morning, once she was alone at home, Robyn got the stepladders out. She placed the new packet of biscuits on top of the highest kitchen cupboard, and then replaced the stepladders in the shed.

'I will not get those ladders out again,' she vowed.

She kept her vow. But two hours later, she found herself poking at the high cupboard with a broom – just out of interest, to see if it would reach.

It did. The biscuits rolled off the cupboard and crashed onto the floor.

'Oh, help,' said Robyn, looking at the squashed packet. 'I can't feed those to Craig. Now I'll have to go and buy some more.'

Meanwhile, there was no point wasting all those broken biscuits...

Next day, she put the new pack inside a strong plastic bag, took it down to the end of the garden, and left it there under the roses.

A few hours later, her feet somehow carried her outside. After all, it was important to stretch her legs now and then, and get some fresh air. And while she was in the garden, she might as well just check on those biscuits.

She looked down at them and gasped. 'What happened?' The pack was shredded. Crumbs and bits of plastic were strewn all over the grass. Then, hearing a rustle in the birch tree, she looked up.

There sat a squirrel nibbling half a chocolate biscuit, with a very smug expression.

After letting it know exactly what she thought of it, Robyn marched down to the shop to buy some more. This time she shut the new packet safely in the greenhouse, where birds and squirrels couldn't reach.

Unfortunately, the sun could. When longing overcame Robyn in the middle of the afternoon, she crept out to the greenhouse, ripped open the pack – and was instantly smeared with molten chocolate.

'Yuck!' said Robyn, tossing the packet of biscuits in the fridge. They would be edible soon enough.

But an hour later they had glued themselves together. She vainly tried to prise them apart before giving up, and plodding to the shop to buy some more.

She didn't mention all these extra packs to Craig. Instead, she racked her brains for a foolproof hiding place.

On Saturday she proudly told her husband, 'I've found the perfect place to keep the chocolate biscuits! They're locked in the medicine cabinet, behind the cough mixture. And to make sure I can't get at them, I want you to look after the key.' She handed it over to Craig.

'You've done well this week!' he said approvingly. 'I'm sure you've lost weight.'

'Mm,' said Robyn. Certainly her waistband wasn't quite as tight as it had been. That was probably due to all those walks to the shop to buy more chocolate biscuits.

'You see, all you needed was some will-power!' Craig told her. 'Don't worry, I'll keep this key safe.' He put it in his pocket.

Robyn was sorting out the laundry when she heard the crash. She ran into the bathroom.

'Are you all right?'

Craig stood there surrounded by bits of broken glass. There was a strong smell of cough medicine.

'Sorry about the mess,' he muttered. 'I was just trying to get, um…'

'A chocolate biscuit?'

He looked sheepish. 'I don't know what came over me. I just felt this overwhelming urge.'

Robyn nodded sympathetically. 'I know. Tell you what – after we've cleared up here, we can have a biscuit with a cup of coffee.'

'No, we can't,' he groaned. 'They fell into the shower.'

They both looked at the shower, which was full of soggy crumbs.

'I'd better drive to the shop and buy some more,' sighed Craig.

But Robyn laughed. 'No, you won't! We'll walk down there together, just like I've been doing all week.'

'You have?'

'I have. And I feel great. I get there faster every day. You see – that proves it. Chocolate biscuits are truly good for us!'

The Good Luck Stone

Connor came hurtling out of the school gate.

'Mum, Mum, I've got you a present!' he cried on seeing Mandy. 'It's a lucky stone! I found it at playtime.'

'That's great! I could do with a bit of luck right now.'

Mandy took the pebble that her seven year old son held out. It was a grey, unremarkable oval, smooth and cool to her hand.

'I know it's lucky,' Connor insisted, 'because straight after I found it I scored a brilliant goal!'

'In that case, I'll make sure to keep it safe,' promised Mandy, ruffling his hair.

'And tomorrow I'll take it with me when I go and see about that new job.'

She smiled down at him, wondering if he'd been picking up signs of her anxiety about her interview. Even though she'd tried to hide her worries, she thought that Connor had probably realised something was amiss.

Watching her son run ahead, she sighed.
It wasn't their lack of money that was the problem, although that was tough. No; the real problem was Russell. Her normally cheerful husband had become distant and withdrawn. It was impossible to talk to him.

Mandy made allowances. She knew Russell was under stress at work, with all that overtime... but then why was there no extra money coming in?

Sometimes, when he was working late, she tried to ring him – but to no avail.

His phone was turned off.

At home, however, Russell checked his phone frequently when he thought she wasn't looking. And the other night, he'd been on the computer long after she'd gone to bed.

'Had to send an important email,' he said, on realising she was still awake.

'At this time of night?'

'For work,' he snapped. Mandy asked no further questions.

She told herself that Russell would never have an affair. It wasn't in his character. If he was aloof and bad-tempered, it was surely because he was worried about money.

If only she could get this job tomorrow, it would take the pressure off him.

Or if her secret fears were to be realised, she thought reluctantly, and their marriage was heading for the rocks, then a job would help. It would give her a new start... Her fingers tightened around Connor's stone.

'Bring me good luck,' she whispered. Whatever happened, somehow she would have to cope – for Connor's sake.

* * *

Next morning Mandy went for the interview with the stone in her handbag. Two hours later she phoned Russell, brimming with excitement.

'I got the job! I can start next week! They need someone to work school hours – it's perfect!'

'That's good,' he said flatly. 'Gotta go. We're busy.'

Mandy's joy ebbed away. Russell hadn't cared. He wasn't even happy for her; although only last year, he would have been whooping at her good luck.

Good luck... As she replaced the phone in her bag, she touched the lucky stone that lay in there. Well, at least Connor would be happy that his gift had worked. And with her first pay-check only weeks away, she decided to celebrate.

So, at the supermarket, she added some treats to the usual shopping. She was carrying her laden shopping bags across the car park when she saw a van nearby start to reverse.

The driver hadn't seen a push-chair standing in its path. The baby's mother was loading her car with her back turned. Mandy dropped her bags and flung herself at the pushchair, shoving it aside.

The van missed it – and her – by inches.
Instead, it drove over her shopping bags
with a loud and drawn-out crunch.

'It was such good luck that I was there,'
she told her family that evening. 'Imagine
what could have happened to that poor baby
if I hadn't seen the van!'

'What did the baby's mummy say?' asked
Connor, wide-eyed.

'She thanked me about a hundred times.
And the van driver apologised a thousand
times, and then insisted on paying for my
squashed shopping. You should have seen
the car park – covered in cornflakes!'

Connor giggled, but Russell didn't even smile.

'Then the supermarket manager gave me
a voucher, and then the baby's mummy
bought me a bunch of flowers!'

'My stone gave you good luck,' said Connor proudly. 'I told you it would! It made you get the job as well. It gave me good luck too – my dinosaur picture got a gold star today.'

'That's because you're good at drawing,' laughed Mandy.

'It's because I had the lucky stone in my pocket yesterday when I drew it,' Connor corrected her.

'Let's see this lucky stone,' said Russell suddenly. He'd hardly spoken until then. He turned the grey pebble in his fingers before handing it back without comment.

'It really is lucky, Daddy,' Connor told him.

'Well, it certainly was today!' agreed Mandy.

'I'm going to put it here to bring the house good luck,' said Connor.

He trotted over to place the stone on the mantelpiece beside Mandy's favourite photo.

Next day, Mandy was dusting when she noticed that the stone was missing. At first she was puzzled.

Then she smiled. Connor must have decided to take it in to school again. No doubt he was hoping to win yet more gold stars…

* * *

As he left work at the day's end, Russell touched the stone deep in his pocket.

Some people that he knew swore by lucky numbers, lucky colours, lucky rituals. He'd never bothered with any of those – at first. He was just naturally lucky. He'd always had an eye for a winner at the betting shop. And when he first tried online poker, he'd won most of the time.

Then things had changed. At first his losses had been small. He needed to recoup them, and bet bigger. He was bound to win this time – wasn't he? Surely it was his turn now.

Instead, he lost, and lost again. This month his losses had been huge. But with one big win, he could still be back on track. Mandy needn't know. She had never spotted a thing.

She wouldn't notice that the lucky stone was missing from the mantelpiece. Russell had taken it because today he needed all the luck that he could get.

The poker wasn't doing it for him any more. Now he entered the betting shop and nodded at the familiar face behind the counter, before he turned to the machines.

The odds weren't good enough on the horses. He touched the lucky stone again, and began playing electronic roulette.

And three minutes later, there it was.
The big win.

Russell stared at the screen, stupefied. His
heart was pounding. Exhilaration made his
skin tingle and his head buzz. He felt as if
he was floating somewhere up by the ceiling.

He'd done it! He'd won at last – and more
than he'd ever won before! The lucky stone
had worked. He'd cleared his debts – most
of them, at least.

Just one more win and he could pay off all
his credit cards. He'd have money to spare.
His worries would be over. Today, with the
lucky stone in his pocket, he couldn't lose!

He laid his bet.

* * *

'You're late home, Russell. More overtime?
I'll get your tea.'

'Wait,' he said. Mandy stopped and looked at him, concerned. 'I've got something to tell you.'

Here it comes, she thought. Is it an affair? Or has he just lost interest in our marriage?

She tried to brace herself, looking at him steadily. Russell did not speak for a moment.

Then he took a pebble from his pocket and rolled it between cold fingers. He needed luck again just now.

'I took this lucky stone to work today.' His voice was hoarse. 'And then I took it to the bookies.'

She stood very still. 'The betting shop?'

'I had a big win there. Huge.' He saw her eyes widen, before he went on rapidly. 'And then I lost it. I lost it all.

And more, and more. I couldn't stop.
I was crazy, for the moment. I thought
I could win it back–' His voice broke.

'You've been gambling,' Mandy said
incredulously. She'd never thought it could
be anything like this. Now she struggled to
grasp it. 'All this time, you've been gambling
our money away. You've been gambling and
losing for months, haven't you?'

All he could do was nod.

'I knew something was up. How **could** you?'

Russell looked at the floor.

'Connor's gone without new clothes, new
toys,' she said, her voice rising. 'I've
scrimped and saved and mended and made
do. I had an egg for tea last night so that
you could have the meat. I didn't mind,
because I thought we had a partnership.'

He couldn't speak. He couldn't think of anything to say.

Mandy's face twisted in grief. 'And you don't even care about the effect on us! How could you be so selfish? Well, I can tell you now, Connor's not going to grow up with an addict for a father. And I'm not going to live with one. Russell, this is the end!'

* * *

As he walked along the dreary road, Russell shoved his hands deep in his pockets. His fingers met cold stone.

Some lucky stone, he thought. Look where it had landed him: penniless and on the street.

Mandy had made him go. He plodded on reluctantly. He was a long way from home now: he didn't know this part of town.

He'd been afraid that she would chuck him out for good. After that first outburst, she'd turned away and wept over the sink. He hadn't known what to say or do. His tongue seemed to have become as mute and heavy as this stone.

And then she'd turned back round. She'd hugged him, sat him down and made him talk.

He'd told her everything. It was a grim relief to finally have it in the open – even though he felt sick and weak with shame.

Now there was more shame to come. Russell stopped, gritting his teeth.

This must be the building. It didn't say Gamblers Anonymous on the door, but Mandy had told him this was the place.

He paused on the doorstep. Could he put himself through this?

He had already put his wife and son through worse. They deserved better. He remembered Mandy's words, just before he'd left.

'The gambling has to end. Connor mustn't have an addict for a father. But I know you can do it, Russell. And I'll support you all the way,' she'd said, and kissed him.

I'm so lucky to have them both, thought Russell. I'm so lucky that they love me in spite of my mistakes.

His fingers found Connor's stone, and held it tight. For Connor; and for Mandy.

I'll make this the luckiest day of all our lives, he promised silently.

Then he squared his shoulders and walked in.

A Slippery Customer

'Now, now,' said Sergeant Kate MacDonald, putting a reassuring arm around the sobbing girl's shoulders. It seemed a huge drama to make over a pet snake: she glanced curiously at the striped corpse lying on the floor.

Andrea had been hysterical when she arrived. Her husband had dialled 999, and Kate and her assistant, PC Mike Fitton, were on the scene in minutes.

They found the living-room in disarray. Apart from the dead snake, chairs were overturned, pot-plants upset, and a brick lay on the floor beneath the open window.

Kate looked around with interest. On the long table stood a large tank which held some branches and a water bowl.

Its lid had been removed and lay on the table next to it, along with two small cages containing rustling straw.

'What exactly happened?' she asked the couple.

'There was a strange man! I was so scared!' Andrea hiccupped. She presented a marked contrast to her husband, thought Kate, noting the girl's careful make-up and stylish hair. Wearing a designer sweat-suit, she clutched a plastic bottle of expensive water in one manicured hand, while the other clutched her husband's arm.

Rupert, scruffy and abrupt, made no attempt to comfort her. Instead, he shook her off to peer gloomily into the snake's tank.

'I was upstairs working on my zoology thesis,' he said gruffly, 'when I heard Andrea scream.'

'So you ran straight down?'

'No. I was in the middle of a tricky paragraph, and I thought it was just a mouse.'

'A mouse?' repeated Kate.

Rupert pointed to the rustling cages. 'We keep mice here to feed the snake. Sometimes they escape. Andrea's afraid of mice.' His lip curled.

'It wasn't a mouse!' protested Andrea tearfully. 'It was a man! I had just got back from the gym, and when I came into the room he was standing there with the snake in his hand!'

'What happened?'

'He clubbed it with a – a cosh. Then he ran for the window, and climbed out before I could do anything. I was terrified!'

Her fear sounded genuine enough, thought Kate.

PC Mike Fitton inspected the window. 'No obvious footprints,' he reported, 'but there could be fingerprints on the frame.'

Andrea shook her head. 'There won't be. He was wearing gloves.'

'Could you describe him?' asked Kate.

'Not really. He had a balaclava on. He was tall and dressed in black.'

'Did he speak, or touch you?' asked Kate gently.

'No.' Andrea was shivering convulsively. Taking gulps of water, she looked over appealingly at her husband: but he was scowling at the corpse.

'Did you see this man, sir?' Kate asked him.

'Unfortunately not. But I've a good idea of who it was. You see, this was a rare king snake with most unusual patterning.
I believe the intruder was a fellow herpetologist.'

'A herp–?' began Mike.

'A specialist in snakes,' supplied Kate. She studied the dead snake: it was certainly very handsome. 'Can you suggest a name?' she asked.

'I could suggest several,' answered Rupert, 'all members of the reptile society.'

'All reptiles,' murmured Andrea.

'But why would they kill it?'

'Jealousy,' Rupert declared.

'They're an obsessive lot,' sighed Andrea.

Kate was sceptical. 'Really? Obsessive enough to break in, force open the tank...'

'The lid wasn't locked,' grunted Rupert. 'It was only held down with that brick. And some stupid person had left the window open so that anyone could get in.' He glared at Andrea.

'Well, I'm sorry for trying to air the room! Your animals smell,' she cried.

'That snake was valuable!'

Mike interrupted diplomatically. 'The window needn't have been wide open to attract an opportunist burglar. Maybe someone climbed in, was curious about the snake, and took it out of the tank. Then it tried to bite him, so he clubbed it.'

'It wouldn't hurt anyone,' objected Rupert.

'It's a **snake**,' said Andrea vehemently.
'You don't get it, do you? People hate
snakes!'

Kate, foreseeing an argument, said swiftly,
'While don't you both go and have a cup of
tea while we look around?'

'Mine's two sugars,' Mike added with a grin.
Once they were alone, he said, 'Well? Shall
I call in the scene of crime officers, Sarge?'

'For a dead snake?' Kate grimaced.
'That'll thrill them no end. No, I think we'll
check out the crime scene ourselves.'

She knelt to scrutinise the snake's body.
'It's been clubbed all right, poor thing.
It's been hit repeatedly with something
smooth and blunt. Quite a frantic attack.'

'Not surprising, if our burglar was scared of getting bitten.'

'Those overturned plants and chairs look as if he thrashed around in panic. But a herpetologist wouldn't be panicked by a snake, would he?' Kate stood up. 'Does this look like the work of a snake lover, Mike?'

'Looks more like a snake hater to me.'

'Quite. Just a common or garden burglar, then?' mused Kate.

'Rupert's not very nice to his wife, is he?' commented Mike as he inspected the tank. 'He didn't exactly rush downstairs to see why she was screaming.'

'No. He didn't seem too shocked at all. I wonder if this valuable snake's insured?'

'Why? You think Rupert might have arranged for its demise?'

'He was unusually quick to finger his envious rivals,' remarked Kate. 'I think he's a slippery customer.'

'Talking of slippery customers – what do you make of this, Sarge?' Mike pointed to the tank's lid.

Kate looked closely. 'A long scrape mark, with brick dust in the scratches,' she observed. 'As if the brick that was holding down the lid slid off... Mike, I think this snake forced its own way out.'

'Would it be strong enough?'

'It's a metre of pure muscle.' Kate nodded at the mice. 'Maybe it went looking for lunch.'

'So our burglar climbs in,' recounted Mike, 'meets a runaway snake, panics and clubs it? Now that's feasible.'

'Yes.' She frowned. 'I just don't think it's very likely. It's a huge coincidence – a masked burglar climbing in just as the snake gets out.'

'Back to our rogue herpetologists, then? Or an insurance scam?'

Kate shook her head thoughtfully. 'Neither. We're missing something, Mike – like a murder weapon.'

'Andrea said the attacker used a cosh. He must have taken it with him.'

'Hmm.' Kate gazed around. 'Well, there's nothing resembling a cosh in here. You'd better check the garden. I'm going to ask our pair a few more questions.'

'And ask them about that cup of tea, Sarge. I'm thirsty.'

'Thirsty?' Kate's head jerked up. 'Mike – that's it! Quick! Come on!'

She hurried from the room and burst into the kitchen. 'Stop right there!' she commanded.

Rupert froze, the kettle in his hand: his wife was running the tap.

'I said **stop**!'

'I'm only washing up,' protested Andrea.

With three strides Kate had crossed the room to Andrea, who gasped and dropped the empty water-bottle.

'Bag up that bottle!' Kate told Mike. 'That's our murder weapon.'

'Are you mad?' cried Rupert. 'That bottle weighs nothing!'

'It's empty now,' said Kate. 'But when it was full of water, it made a very effective cosh. If those smears on it are snake blood–'

'What are you saying?'

Kate looked at Andrea. 'Your wife came in and found the snake had escaped from its tank. She panicked and clubbed it with her bottle.'

'Never!'

'Then she invented the intruder because she knew you would be furious with her. And she drank the water so that we wouldn't identify the bottle as the weapon.'

'Don't be ridiculous,' snapped Rupert. 'That snake was a pet!'

But Andrea spoke up, her voice shaking.
'It was hiding in the plants. I heard it hissing.
I was terrified.'

'You know it wouldn't have hurt you!'

'It came straight at me! I've never been so
scared. I loathed that snake,' cried Andrea.

'What?' Rupert looked stunned.

'I've tried to tell you, but you were obsessed
with it. You loved that snake more than you
loved me.'

'That's not true!'

'It is. Today you've proved it.' Andrea
thrust her hands at Kate. 'Go on, arrest me.
Put on the handcuffs!'

But Kate said calmly, 'I'm not arresting
anybody – not even for wasting police time.

I suggest that you two need to have a long talk with each other. Let's go, Constable.'

Outside, Mike muttered, 'So Rupert was harbouring a viper in his bosom?'

Kate shook her head compassionately.
'No, just an unhappy wife. The killer was a jealous rival, sure enough; but not the one he thought.'

'He's a slippery customer, all right,' said Mike.

'Maybe in future he'll be a little less cold-blooded than his poor old snake! Come on, Mike – let's go and find that cup of tea.'

Pass the Cake

Teresa rang the doorbell and waited apprehensively.

Finally the door opened. Leaning on her stick, Elsie looked out with a disapproving frown.

'Oh!' she said. 'I thought you'd be a salesman.' But despite seeing her neighbour at the door, the frown stayed on her face.

'Hallo, Elsie! Don't worry, I haven't come to borrow anything...' Her heart sinking, Teresa realised that this was a bad idea. Her elderly neighbour had never been friendly. Elsie preferred to keep herself to herself.

However, Teresa reminded herself that she was doing this for Maisie. So she held out the large, round object in her hands and said, 'It's a present for you, Elsie. It's a cake.'

'A present?' said Elsie blankly.

'It's from our daughter Maisie. She loves baking. She can do it from her wheelchair. There aren't many things that – well. Anyway, we decided to make this for you.'

Teresa put the cake, wrapped in cling-film, on the table by the door. Elsie peered at it suspiciously. It was decorated with red and yellow birds cut out of icing.

'Well, I'd better get back to Maisie.' Teresa escaped next door to her daughter.

'Did Elsie like it?' asked Maisie eagerly. Teresa smiled and kissed her nine-year-old's pale cheek.

'She looked quite stunned,' she said. 'I'm sure she'll love it. Shall we go out into the garden now, and see how those birds are doing?'

She wheeled Maisie outside. There were so few things that Maisie could enjoy; bird watching was one of them. Mixing that cake had been a struggle. Even reading tired her.

Her treatment seemed to be endless. Sometimes Teresa longed for a sign from heaven that it was working.

But she knew she had to trust the doctors, who assured her that the test results were good. Meanwhile the most important thing was to keep Maisie smiling.

'No birds today,' said Maisie dolefully, scanning the empty garden. Teresa silently blamed Elsie's cat, which lurked in these gardens, frightening all the bird-life away.

'You know what Elsie's doing right now?' she said, to distract Maisie. 'She's taking an enormous bite of your cake – and saying, MMM! That is so delicious! What a cake!'

* * *

'What a cake,' said Elsie scornfully. How on earth was she supposed to eat that massive thing? It was ridiculous. And as for all that coloured icing – it would bring on her heartburn.

She might as well throw the cake away. It wasn't as if she ever had friends around to share it with. Her neighbour had just thrust it at her, giving her no chance to say no!

Giving her no chance to say thank you either. Elsie leaned on her stick, gazing at the cake and thinking of the quiet little girl next door. Had it really been made especially for her? It was the first present that she'd had in ages.

When the doorbell rang again, her heart gave an odd leap. If this was Teresa, maybe she could thank her after all – even if she didn't want that cake.

'Oh, it's you,' she said curtly, letting in the handyman, Clive, who had come to fix her light fitting.

'Yes, it's me,' he said, cheerfully unfazed. He never expected much of a greeting from Elsie.

The task didn't take Clive long. 'That light's safe now,' he said as he folded up his ladder. 'Anything else need doing?'

'No, that was all... But do you want a cup of tea?' asked Elsie.

Then she wondered what on earth had got into her. Clive had done several little jobs for her before without needing cups of tea. She'd never encouraged him to hang around. So she didn't know whether to be relieved or disappointed when he shook his grey head with a smile.

'Thanks, but I'd better get on. I've got another job just down the street.'

On impulse, Elsie picked up the cake. 'Here,' she said, 'take this. I can't eat it. It'll give me indigestion.'

'No, no! You've already paid me,' Clive protested.

'Not enough,' said Elsie. 'Don't think I don't know. You undercharge me. Take it as a present in return for all that work.'

Clive's face was red as he backed out of the door, clutching the cling-filmed cake.

'Well, thank you,' he said. What a strange old lady! he reflected. She'd always seemed a bit of a dragon, but maybe she wasn't as cantankerous as he'd thought. Next time he was passing, he'd drop in and have that cup of tea.

His next job was a few houses down: a washing machine that needed fixing. Clive carried the cake in and put it down carefully on the kitchen work-top.

'Cake!' shouted the toddler who had run in to inspect him.

'Not yours, Billy,' said his mother wearily. 'Keep out of the way, now.'

'He's no trouble,' said Clive. He was perfectly happy to have Billy playing round his feet while he worked.

'Can you pass me that big spanner? You make a great little helper,' he told him. 'You're just the same age as my grandson. Mind you, he lives right across the country.'

'Do you see much of him?' asked Billy's mum.

'Not enough,' said Clive ruefully.

'I'm sure he must miss you.'

At her sympathetic tone, he found himself telling her all about his three grandchildren and their latest exploits. She laughed as he showed her a photo of the go-kart that they'd tried to build from cardboard boxes.

The washing machine was soon fixed. When Billy's mum paid Clive, he couldn't help noticing how tired she looked. He held the cake out to her. 'Here, you have this.'

'Me?'

Clive laughed. 'I daresay young Billy here will help you out with eating it! It was an unexpected present from a customer. But the thing is, my wife's on a low-fat diet. It wouldn't be fair on her if I took this home.'

'Well – thanks,' she said, some of the tired lines on her face disappearing as she smiled.

'Cake!' yelled Billy gleefully. Clive waved at him as he walked down the path. He vowed that he'd go and see his grandchildren soon: he'd make the effort, instead of waiting for them to visit. At least he'd left a happy two-year-old behind.

* * *

'Oh, Lord,' said Billy's mum, Maxine. 'What can I do with this?'

It wasn't that nice handyman's fault. He wasn't to know that Billy could only eat gluten-free.

'We'll keep this cake for Dad,' she told Billy, 'and you can have one of your special biscuits. Okay?'

'Okay,' said Billy obediently. Maxine hugged him.

'Bless you,' she said.

It was so hard sometimes with Dan working away... but that handyman had made her realise just how lucky she was to have Billy. And at least Dan was home every weekend.

Still, now that she thought about it, the cake would probably be stale before he next came home.

'I know; let's go and see Anna,' she told Billy. 'We can give her the cake.'

'Daddy's cake!'

'I've remembered that Daddy likes ice-cream best, just like you. So the cake can be Anna's.'

'Anna's cake!' Billy beamed. He had grown very attached to his new child-minder.

Anna only lived round the corner, but looked surprised to see them on the doorstep.

Maxine hadn't paid her a purely social call before.

'I'm sorry – I can't take Billy now,' said Anna falteringly. 'I've got two babies with me.' Her English was already much better than it had been when she started looking after Billy.

'It's all right,' Maxine reassured her, 'that's not why I've come. I just thought you might like to have this cake.'

'Oh!' said Anna wonderingly.

'Just to say Thank you,' said Maxine, 'for being so good with Billy. He's been really happy with you.'

She felt guilty about how stand-offish she'd been with Anna at first, wondering if she should trust a foreigner with her little boy. But now she thought she'd like to get to know Anna better.

It must be lonely for her sometimes, with only tiny tots for company. Maxine knew from experience how difficult that could be...

Anyway, she was glad she'd found a good home for the cake.

'I won't stop now,' she said, 'you're busy. But we'll see you tomorrow!'

As they left, Anna carried the cake inside, wondering what to do with it. It was a shame she couldn't give it to the babies she was looking after.

But even though it looked delicious, there was no knowing what was in it: and one of the babies had a nut allergy, while the other had a very fussy mother. As for Anna herself, she didn't care for sweet things.

All the same, the gift made her feel good.

British people weren't so stiff once you got to know them. Maxine was much friendlier than she had seemed at first. And it was nice to be told that she was doing her job well.

The cake would not be wasted. Anna smiled down at the babies.

'This is a very special cake,' she told them. 'Shall I show you what we're going to do with it? We're going to give the birds a treat!'

She carried the pair of babies out into the garden, where they lay on a blanket and watched with interest as she broke the cake in pieces and put the crumbs on saucers. The icing was too rich for birds, she thought; so she left it on the patio.

After she had laid the saucers out around the garden, she still had half the cake left over.

There was a bird-table in the garden backing on to hers – the one where she'd sometimes seen the poor girl in the wheelchair. But nobody was in the garden now, so stepping over the low fence, she piled the bird-table high with cake crumbs.

'There,' she said to the babies. 'Shall we be very quiet and see what happens?'

* * *

Maisie was dozing in her wheelchair. She stretched and smiled as Teresa came in.

'I just dreamt that I was flying, Mum! I felt so strong! I'd grown a hundred wings.'

'Well, that would be a novelty,' laughed Teresa. 'Goodness, what's that noise?'

There was a commotion going on outside the window. Maisie's eyes widened as she stared out at the garden. 'Oh, Mum!' she cried.

'That must be what woke me. Look!'

Finches and blue-tits crowded round the bird-table. In the air above, more birds swooped and fluttered. Tweets and chirrups filled their garden, and the one behind.

Maisie clapped her hands excitedly. 'Oh, how wonderful! Birds everywhere – it's just like my dream!' Her face was shining with delight.

Teresa laid her hands on her daughter's shoulders and gazed out at the fluttering throng. She was bewildered. Where had these birds all come from? And where was Elsie's greedy cat?

She could not guess that, having stolen all the red and yellow icing, it was lying down behind the shed and feeling rather sick.

She only knew that, like a sign from heaven, the air was full of wings.

The Ghost Upstairs

'I'm afraid it's a little bit out-dated,' sighed the agent.

Viv raised an eyebrow. 'Out-dated? Well, that's one word for it!' **Ruin** was another. The big Victorian pub, stripped of its fixtures, looked gloomy and dilapidated. Somehow it had survived the war when half the town got flattened. But the recession had finally done for it.

It was certainly run-down, thought Viv; but there was more than enough space – and it was cheap. She began to feel excited.

'There are living quarters upstairs, aren't there?' she asked.

'In theory, yes. But no-one's lived up there for years.'

Up the narrow stairs, an old iron bedstead still squatted in a large room, with the yellowed remnants of an ancient quilt thrown over it. The paper was peeling off the walls, and the uneven floor creaked ominously.

'No heating up here,' confessed the agent. 'But plenty of storage. And there's enough space downstairs for a ballroom.'

Viv laughed. 'Well, I love to dance! But I was thinking of a workshop.' She was already planning where to put the girls and their sewing machines. Her own premises at last! She glowed with pride. It had been a long journey since those tough days after her divorce, when she started up the fancy dress business in her bedroom.

It had been a warmer bedroom than this one, thank goodness! She shivered, suddenly aware of a freezing draught that swept through the room.

It didn't matter. Viv had her own flat, and didn't need to live here. This upstairs room was just for storage. So she declared, 'I'll take it!'

A few weeks later, everything was up and running. The sewing machines were whirring busily when Viv bounced in waving a sheet of paper.

'Good news! We've just got a big order for a Cinderella themed wedding. They want ball-gowns, Prince Charming's outfit, footmen's uniforms – the works!'

'Excellent!' said Malika. 'That'll keep us busy for a while.'

'I've got just the right material upstairs.'

Viv ran up to the bedroom. This was a great start to her new premises – just the boost her business needed.

Upstairs, rolls of fabric were stacked against the walls. Plastic boxes full of trimmings were piled on the old iron bedstead, which had proved too heavy to shift. The sun streamed through the window as Viv hunted for the bolt of pale pink satin. But seconds later, a chilly draught whirled round her, as if she'd just opened a freezer door.

Viv shook her head in irritation. How could anyone have lived up here? Hot one minute, freezing cold the next.

Carrying the roll of fabric back downstairs, she asked, 'How about this for Cinderella's dress?'

'Perfect!' Leila stroked the satin admiringly, and then shivered and rubbed her arms. 'Ooh, it's just gone chilly in here.'

'The draughts in this place are terrible!' agreed Viv.

But she couldn't work out where the cold air was coming from. It seemed to shift as she walked around the workshop.

'I'll sort it out,' she promised her machinists. 'You need to be warmer than this.'

However, a couple of electric heaters from the local hardware shop failed to fix the problem. No matter which part of the workshop Viv was in, moments later she would start to shiver. She was always cold in there. Upstairs was even worse.

So Viv returned to the hardware store, where the owner, Andy, greeted her with a smile.

'Did the heaters not do the trick? I guess that old pub must take some warming up.'

'They work fine, thanks – but the draughts in the building are dreadful! Have you got any draught-proofing strip?'

Andy rummaged on the shelves. 'Here you are – though it might not be proof against the ghost.'

'What ghost?' asked Viv.

He grinned. 'The ghost upstairs! It was common knowledge when I used to drink in that pub. We'd hear these strange creaking noises overhead.'

'All old buildings creak,' Viv pointed out sceptically.

'Sure. It was a standing joke, but some of the old guys took it quite seriously.'

'Whose ghost was it supposed to be?'

Andy shook his head. 'I couldn't tell you. Old Ron the landlord said nobody had lived up there for thirty years. He got quite snappy when we asked him.'

'Hmm,' said Viv. 'So did anyone actually see this ghost? After a few pints, perhaps?'

Andy laughed. 'No sightings, only creaks and groans. Still, it makes a good story!'

'It certainly does.' Back at the dilapidated old pub, Viv recounted it to the girls.

'Ooh!' said Leila. 'How creepy. And that ceiling **does** creak. I can believe there's something spooky up there!'

'Well, I can't,' said Viv dampeningly. 'I don't believe in ghosts.' She finished applying the last length of draught-proofing strip to the doorway, and straightened up. 'There! That should keep the cold out.'

Even as she spoke, a sudden chill alighted round her shoulders, settling on her like a shawl of freezing fog. Viv took a sharp breath. But no-one else had noticed.

'That feels better already,' commented Leila. Her arms were bare – and not goose-pimpled as Viv's now were. Viv gave herself a shake. This talk of ghosts was making her imagine things. How ridiculous! She went over to her table and concentrated on her design for Cinderella's gown.

They were making good progress with the wedding costumes. The Ugly Sisters' dresses were already half finished; Viv carried them upstairs to hang over the old bedstead. It was freezing cold up there too.

But it was not until that evening, as she pored over her accounts at home, that she finally stretched and sat back – and realised that she had been cold all day. She went into her bedroom for a jumper. Although the room felt warm when she walked in, seconds later her teeth were chattering.

Viv stood still for a moment.

Then she shook her head, donned her jumper and turned up her heating.

'Must be going down with flu,' she muttered. No doubt she'd wake up feverish in the morning.

Next day, Viv felt fine – but cold. Perhaps the heating was playing up. She carried a thermometer around her flat and watched the temperature drop in room after room. It must be the weather, she decided.

Outside, it was clear and bright; the sunshine seemed to dispel the chill that had settled on her. Yet as soon as she entered the workshop in the old pub, she felt freezing once again.

'Malika? Are you girls warm enough?'

'Sure,' replied Malika. 'The building must be heating up in this sunshine. It's been creaking like mad all morning.'

'Strange,' muttered Viv, as she trudged upstairs to fetch the Ugly Sisters' costumes.

They lay on the floor of the upstairs room in a dusty, crumpled heap. The flounces which she'd tacked on yesterday had come adrift.

'What on earth?' Viv picked them up and shook them out. A breeze must have blown them down from their hook over the bed – yet where could a breeze have come from? The window was jammed shut.

Standing with the dresses in her arms, Viv felt a wave of frozen air lap round her. The floorboards creaked and groaned beneath her feet. **The ghost**...

What nonsense! All the same, she ran downstairs in a hurry.

'I'll be back in a bit,' she told the girls, before heading off to the hardware shop.

She didn't know who else to ask round here but Andy. Breathlessly she said,

'Where does the old landlord of the pub live? You said you knew him.'

He looked at her with some concern. 'Yes, I do. Are you all right, Viv?'

'I'm okay. But the building isn't. It's got – some problems that I need to discuss.'

Andy nodded. 'That doesn't surprise me. Apart from knocking down a wall or two, Ron didn't exactly spend a fortune on the place. I'll write his address down for you. It's not far away.'

'Then I'll go there now,' she said with resolution.

'Viv? If there's anything I can help you out with, let me know,' he offered.

'Thanks,' she said gratefully, although she couldn't possibly tell him what was on her mind. **I think the place is haunted...**
It was a laughable idea. All the same, she was determined to find out what she could.

At Ron's house, the door was opened by a stout man in his sixties who greeted her suspiciously.

'If there's anything wrong with the old pub, I don't want to know. I'm done with the place. Speak to the letting agent,' he growled.

'Wait! Just one question,' pleaded Viv before he could close the door on her. 'Who lived there before you?'

'I never lived there. It was my aunt Ivy who inherited it from my Grandad. She lived there for years – the horrible old witch.'

'Witch?' Viv was startled.

'Yes, witch! She was a selfish, mean old woman. She never did a stroke of work.' Rob's face was thunderous. 'She stayed in her bed all day like Lady Muck and had everyone running up and down for her non-stop. She treated my mum like a skivvy! Her own sister!'

'But–'

The words poured out in a tide of pent-up bitterness. 'And she treated me like a servant! I hated Ivy. That pub's been in the family seventy years. Now it's nothing. Ivy cursed it.'

'Whatever do you mean?'

'After she died, she turned the beer. Frightened off the customers. Ruined the business. I had to close down. She was a useless old woman, and she couldn't bear anyone else to succeed.'

'Are you telling me Ivy haunted the place?' demanded Viv.

Ron scowled. 'I'm not saying anything. It's not my problem any more.' He slammed the door.

Viv stared at the closed door, startled by Ron's hatred and vehemence as much as by his words. When she turned to leave, she shivered. The sense of cold had followed her all the way here like a clinging shadow.
But now she could put a name to it....
Ivy. The pub's very own Ugly Sister.

As she pulled her jacket round her goose-pimpled shoulders, a thought came to her.
It wasn't just the old pub that was haunted.
It was **her**.

* * *

Viv was distracted.

She mislaid the order book, gave Leila the wrong measurements, and had a row over the phone with a sports club about a mascot costume. Everything seemed to be going wrong.

Maybe she was trying to expand too fast...

Or maybe it was Ivy.

Viv didn't want to believe in Ivy. Yet no matter how many woolly layers she wore, she couldn't get warm: while overhead, the ceiling groaned and creaked more painfully than ever.

The girls joked about the flakes of plaster that were shed onto their machines.

'Keep your eyes on your work,' snapped Viv.

They looked surprised. It wasn't like Viv to snap.

But the constant cold was getting her down. It chilled her to the core. It reminded her of all the darkest places in her life: her father's illness, her divorce, her redundancy. It sapped her of all hope and confidence.

She imagined Ivy lurking like a malignant spider in the room upstairs, spinning a grey web of despair, willing her to fail.

Shivering in the workshop at the day's end, Viv remembered how she had blithely said **I don't believe in ghosts...**

Had it only been three weeks ago? Ever since then, this chilly shroud had wrapped itself around her. Maybe this was Ivy's punishment.

I don't believe in ghosts. Well, she did now.

'I was wrong,' she said aloud to the empty building. 'I do believe in ghosts!

Now leave me alone!' But when she locked up and went home, the cold still followed her.

And that was the night the ceiling of the pub fell in.

* * *

The floor was littered with plaster. The machines were covered in a grey layer like a shower of dirty snow.

'At least the bedstead didn't come through the ceiling,' said Malika glumly.

Horrified, Viv stared up at the gaping hole above their heads. 'We can't work in here now! We'll have to close until I've had an engineer in to check the damage.'

'But what about the costumes? The Cinderella ball-gown?' Leila cried.

'That doesn't matter,' said Viv grimly.

'I had an email this morning cancelling the ball-gown. The bride's fallen in love with a traditional wedding dress.' The rest of the Cinderella order still stood; but for how long? It was just one piece of bad luck after another.

They moved the machines into the small back room. But there wasn't space in there to operate them, so Viv sent the girls home.

Then she cautiously mounted the stairs. She knew she shouldn't, for it might be dangerous; but there were expensive costumes there that needed rescuing. She couldn't afford to leave them.

As soon as she stepped into Ivy's room, the biting cold attacked her. Gasping and stumbling in her shock, Viv fell against the bedstead. The floor trembled ominously. Desperately Viv crawled back to the safety of the wall.

She leaned against it, her heart pounding, her fingers already numb with cold. She should have known better than to come up here. Ivy was after her.

Viv closed her eyes, exhausted. She'd never make a go of this business. There were too many setbacks. It was all too hard. She couldn't do it...

Then her eyes snapped open. She hadn't come this far to be defeated by a ghost – especially the ghost of a woman too lazy to even get up out of bed.

'It takes more than this to get the better of me! Do you hear me, Ivy?' she said as she struggled to her feet. 'Like it or not – I'm here to stay!'

* * *

There had to be a way to get rid of Ivy.

Priests and exorcism flitted across Viv's mind; but she didn't know any priests. And somehow it didn't seem the right path to take.

Instead she went down to the hardware store to pick Andy's brains about the place.

'Who used to live in that pub, Andy, back in the days when it was a pub?' she asked. 'I know Ron didn't live there.' She had told Andy about her brief visit to the surly Ron.

'Some old relation lived upstairs, I believe – but she died years ago, before my time. When I started going in there, it was just Ron and his mother Beryl. Ron's always been a bit of a grump but Beryl was a lovely lady. She's still alive: I believe she's in the Beeches Care Home now, not far from here.' He studied Viv with kindly concern. 'Viv, are you okay? You look pretty shaken up.'

'Oh, I'm fine. It's just a temporary setback. We'll soon be back on track, once the engineer's been in.'

And once I get rid of Ivy, she added silently, as she set off to the Beeches Care Home. It was only a couple of miles away.

She hoped she might learn more from Beryl. What exactly, she didn't know: just some clue as to how to get rid of Ivy.

However, her heart sank as she was led into the care home's lounge, where Ron's mother sat huddled in a chair that swamped her. Beryl looked tired and shrunken.

'I'm afraid you may not get much sense out of her,' warned the carer. 'She's very sleepy these days. Beryl, dear! Wake up! You've got a visitor.'

The old lady opened dim, faraway eyes.

'Is it Ron?' she whispered, and slumped deeper into the chair when Viv said no.

'Ron sends you his love,' Viv added. She was rewarded by seeing a smile creep across Beryl's face. 'I'm the new tenant at his pub.'

'The pub? Is it still there?' the old lady murmured.

'It certainly is. Do you remember it? And do you remember your big sister, Ivy?'

Beryl's face clouded. 'Ivy? She's not here, is she?'

'Oh, no!' said Viv, although the chill had accompanied her all the way to the care home.

Trying to ignore it, she asked, 'Ivy used to live upstairs at the pub, didn't she? You ran errands for her.'

'My goodness, yes! All day. She kept me on my toes.' The old lady was waking up now, and becoming more alert.

'That must have been hard,' said Viv sympathetically.

'Oh, I didn't mind. After all, she couldn't do her own running, could she?' Beryl said. 'Not the way she was.'

'Why? How was she?'

'Ever since the war.' The old lady sighed. 'Oh, dear. What terrible times those were. When that bomb fell on the shops in town, Ivy was trapped for two full days before they got her out.'

'What?' Viv was appalled.

'Poor Ivy.' Beryl wiped a rheumy eye.

'It was mid-winter, and she nearly froze under the rubble. Her leg was crushed, poor thing. She spent months in hospital, but after that she couldn't walk properly, and she was always in pain. No wonder she got tetchy. That bomb put paid to all her dreams.'

'What dreams?' asked Viv, bewildered.

'Oh, her business. She'd set it up in the pub, in the upstairs room.'

'Really? What sort of business?'

Beryl smiled, remembering. 'A dance studio. Swing dance was all the rage. You should have seen Ivy doing the Lindy Hop! But she could waltz, too, like a princess. She could do everything. She just loved to dance, did Ivy.'

She began to reminisce about the wartime dances, while Viv listened in astonishment.

Could this Ivy be the witch that Ron had moaned about? Instead, Beryl described a lively, generous sister with boundless energy, who lived for dancing – until a bomb destroyed her dreams...

The old lady's face was alight with memories; but at last she nodded and dozed off.

'Beryl enjoyed your visit,' commented the carer as Viv left. 'I haven't seen her so happy for a while. She's always waiting for her son to visit, and he never does.'

'I'll come again,' Viv promised.

She returned to the pub, her head whirling as madly as a Lindy Hop. There she stood in the gloom amidst the plaster.

'Is this what it felt like underneath the rubble, Ivy?' she said aloud to the emptiness.

'Alone in the cold and dark, facing the end of all your hopes?'

She suddenly remembered the first time she had felt the cold. It had been on that very first day, when the agent showed her round. Viv had been upstairs, standing beside the iron bedstead where Ivy had spent so much of her shattered life.

What had Viv said? Not '**I don't believe in ghosts.**' That had been later.

'**I love to dance.**' Those had been her words. And ever since that moment, the cold had trailed her.

Maybe Ivy didn't hate her after all. Maybe she was just looking for a kindred spirit...

* * *

'That new steel joist has made it safe,' said the engineer. 'It was a simple fix.

But it's only just in time – the whole ceiling could have come down any day.'

'What?' Viv was horrified.

'Whoever took out the supporting wall deserves a kicking. I'm amazed it held up for so long. What made it give way? Somebody jumping around upstairs?'

'There was nobody here at the time.'

'No? Well, at least you got a warning and could fix it before the whole lot fell down,' he said. 'It's safe enough now.'

No thanks to Ron, thought Viv. He'd knocked down the supporting wall. He hadn't looked after the building any better than he'd looked after his beer, his business – or his mother Beryl.

Her workshop could have been buried beneath rubble – if the fall of plaster hadn't alerted her to danger. But Ivy had saved Viv's dreams from being destroyed, as her own had been.

Viv hurried outside to tell the girls they could safely move the machines back in. It was her second piece of good news that day: for the Cinderella wedding group were delighted with their costumes and were to feature in a magazine.

'Great publicity! But what shall we do with Cinderella's ball-gown – the one she didn't want?' asked Malika.

'I'm sure we'll find a use for it,' said Viv. 'In fact, I'll finish it myself.'

So she got to work on Cinderella's gown. At the end of the day, with the last piece of lace sewn on, she carried it upstairs.

Those new floorboards needed a rug, she thought; and the bedstead could do with a prettier cover. She would re-paper the walls, too, when she had more time.

But for now, the ball gown was decoration enough. Carefully she hung it over the old bed.

'This is yours, Ivy,' she said aloud. 'Because you weren't an ugly sister. You were a princess.'

Running back downstairs, she waited for the cold to follow her. But she felt no shivers: no goose-bumps. For the first time in weeks, she was warm.

She wouldn't need to wear her jacket when she met up with Andy later on. He'd bashfully asked her out to dinner, and she'd said yes.

The girls were packing up.

'See you tomorrow, Viv!' said Leila. Then, at a creak overhead, she glanced up in alarm. 'Ooh, what's that? The ceiling's not going to collapse again, is it?'

Viv listened carefully. The faint sounds from the upstairs room were quite regular.

One two three, **one** two three, they went, as if someone as light as a breeze were waltzing up above.

She shook her head and smiled.

'Don't worry! It's all fine up there. That's just our friendly ghost.'

Stage Fright

'We're far too early!' Karen glanced around at the rows of empty chairs set out in the school hall.

'I know. I want to get a good seat.' Steve hurried to the front row and sat down, staring anxiously at the stage.

Karen was amused. What was the big deal? This wasn't exactly Les Mis! It was just a hotch-potch of Little Orphan Annie and a few songs cobbled together by a music teacher.

Then she reminded herself that this was a big deal for Steve – and for Freddie: because this was Freddie's first time on stage.

'I know he's nervous, although he pretended not to be. He's taking this so seriously!

I hope he remembers his lines,' muttered Steve.

Karen pressed his hand. 'He will. Don't worry. You spent long enough practising them together!' Time that could have been spent with me, she thought ruefully.

She sternly banished the thought. She shouldn't be jealous of the hours father and son had spent rehearsing, even if it meant she now knew the lines backwards. There wouldn't be any surprises in this performance.

She studied the program, and read:
Baron Bluebeard – Freddie King.
He was the surly baddie who came good and led the last song with unexpected jollity.

If only, Karen thought grimly, and then chided herself.

She wasn't being fair. She'd only married Steve two months ago, after a whirlwind romance. It wasn't surprising if Freddie was wary of her – even resentful.

Not that he was ever actually rude. But he had put the barriers up. He always wore that aloof, suspicious look. He never smiled at her the way he smiled at Steve.

Karen sighed. She hadn't foreseen how hard it would be, breaking into such a close father-son relationship.

Freddie and Steve had been on their own for five years, since Marie had died. Knowing how much Freddie missed Marie, Karen had tried her best to be warm and friendly.
So far it hadn't worked.

Now the hall was filling up fast. The bustle quietened and the lights went down.
'Here we go,' said Steve tensely.

'He'll be fine, Steve!'

'If the nerves don't get to him.' The nerves had obviously got to Steve, whose hands were knotted together.

A chorus of children's voices sang out as a group of ragged orphans ran on stage. Since Freddie wasn't in this first scene, Karen let her thoughts wander back to her own childhood.

She barely remembered her own father. No plays in the school hall for him: he'd left home when she was only four. Mum had worked so hard to keep everything together that Karen had seldom felt his lack.

But now she wondered if that was why she felt so apart from Steve and Freddie. Theirs was a relationship she'd never known. I don't understand the secret of fatherhood, she thought. And I'm jealous!

She caught her breath at the realisation. Sudden tears pricked at her eyes.

If her father had stayed – would he have come to school plays and cheered her on at netball matches? Would he have taken her skating and teased her about boyfriends and helped her with her homework?

Suddenly, for the first time in years, Karen found herself wishing there had been somebody she could have called Dad.

She shook her head and blinked hard. How silly to start brooding on that now!

Steve sat up straight. 'Here he comes!'

Karen concentrated on the stage. It wouldn't do to miss Freddie's big moment. She gazed up with a fixed smile as he made his entrance.

But this wasn't the self-assured Freddie that she'd come to know. He looked terrified. Not even the black moustache and the fearsome eyebrows could disguise his nervousness. He was supposed to growl his first line at the orphans, but it came out as a croak.

Orphan Annie answered brightly. In answer, Freddie gabbled his next line and tripped over the words. There was none of the fiery conviction that he'd managed in rehearsal.

Karen bit her lip. Please just let Freddie make it through the scene, she prayed.

Orphan Annie piped, 'Don't be so angry with us, Baron!' and waited for Freddie's reply.

It didn't come. Freddie stood as stiff as a rake, his mouth opening and closing silently.

In the embarrassed hush, Karen heard the faint murmur of a prompt, but she couldn't make out the words.

Neither could Freddie. He swallowed and did a bit of stage business with his cane. The audience laughed appreciatively. Well done, Freddie, thought Karen. Don't panic!

She ran frantically through the scene in her head. What was the next line? She'd heard it so many times...

'I can't remember it!' muttered Steve wretchedly.

Freddie's anguished gaze swept out over the audience, and caught Karen's eye. For a moment, their gazes locked in mutual desperation.

Then the words came to Karen. Silently she mouthed:

'Can't you see I'm busy, little girl?' She gave him her most encouraging smile.

'Can't you see I'm busy, little girl?' bellowed Freddie.

'Go, Freddie!' whispered Karen. The play swept onwards, and as line followed line, she saw him gradually relax. He began to swagger and roar and twirl his moustache, while the audience cheered.

'He's really good, isn't he?' whispered Steve. Karen nodded.

At last Freddie's voice rang out amongst the others in the final song. When the cast took their bows, Karen jumped to her feet and clapped enthusiastically.

The music teacher came forward with an endless list of thank-yous.

'...To the school for the use of their hall, and to the wonderful cast of adults and children who have given their time to this fund-raising performance for the NSPCC...'

At last she finished, and Freddie was able to join his family.

'Whew! Thank goodness that's over. That's the first time in sixty years I've ever been on stage, and I sincerely hope it's the last. Never again!' he vowed, but behind the greasepaint his eyes were alight in a way Karen hadn't seen before.

'You were great, Dad!' Steve clapped him on the shoulder. 'Mum would have been proud of you!'

'Do you think Marie would have enjoyed it? I hope so. I nearly dried up at one point, though,' said Freddie, his eyes turning to Karen.

'But you didn't,' she reminded him.
'You kept going.'

'Only just!' said Freddie, and then, to her surprise, he swept her into a mighty hug that almost lifted her off her feet.
'Thanks,' he muttered gruffly.

Karen hugged her father-in-law back.
So this was what it felt like...

'You were brilliant!' she said. 'You were the star of the show, Freddie – I mean – Dad.'

The One That Got Away

'I've got to go.' Ken began to stow away his fishing gear. 'I promised Sue I'd cook the dinner tonight.'

'You're kidding!' said Lyle incredulously. 'She's got you under her thumb, hasn't she? You should have got her trained, the way I've trained Rachel.'

'I'm sure,' said Ken. 'Anyway, I'll see you.'

After his friend left, Lyle stretched out lazily, and reached for another piece of the cake Rachel had packed for him. What a fool Ken was, running round after his wife! Lyle had chosen Rachel as a girlfriend because he knew she wouldn't make demands.

When Lyle met her, she was quiet and shy. It had been easy for him to impress her.

He'd told her he was a champion angler, and flashed a few trophies he'd picked up at a garage sale.

He paid her compliments. Gave her presents. And Rachel fell for him hook, line and sinker.

Now he'd got her safely netted, Lyle was free to do what he liked. A lazy day's fishing suited him well.

Sometimes, though, he spent the day at the races, or in the bookies or the pub. Rachel was none the wiser. She was busy at her job.

Lately he'd had the idea of telling her he was going sea fishing – that would mean whole weekends spent basking by the sea.

He'd have no need to actually board a boat. Lyle didn't like boats; he got dreadfully sea-sick. But he could always fool her by buying a fish or two to bring home.

'I'm the one that got away,' he said to himself smugly.

Now raindrops began to spatter on the water. Lyle swore: he didn't enjoy fishing in the rain. It was time to go. He tried to lift his rod out of the water, and felt a pull.

'It's a big one!' he gasped.

Carefully, he reeled it in. Something heavy was dangling from the hook. It wasn't a fish.

Picking the weed off it, Lyle held it up. It looked like an old tin mug, black with dirt.

He snorted and nearly threw it back. Then he tossed it into his bag. He would give it to Rachel – it would be the first present he had given her for a long time.

'What's this?' asked Rachel when he handed the mug over.

'That's my catch. I nearly got a huge one, though. You should have seen it. This big!' He spread his hands.

Rachel laughed. 'Is that right? It's just as well I'm not relying on you to catch our dinner!'

Lyle was indignant. 'That pond's just too small for proper fishing,' he said huffily. 'There's nothing big left in there. I ought to try a bit of sea fishing some time; that would suit me better.'

'Good idea,' said Rachel. 'So what shall I do with this old mug?'

'Whatever you like. It's for you.'

'Lovely,' she said.

A week later, Lyle came home from a fishing trip that had been mostly spent in the pub. Rachel greeted him with shining eyes.

'Guess what?' she said. 'That mug you fished up is an antique silver tankard! It's worth hundreds. I got it valued, and I've just sold it on the internet!'

'What?'

'Well, you don't think I spend my weekends just waiting around for you to come home, do you?' she replied. 'I've been trading bits and bobs online. But this is my biggest catch by far!'

'Yours? It was **my** big catch!' cried Lyle indignantly.

'You gave it to me,' Rachel pointed out. 'Anyway, I've already spent the money on a two-week holiday in the Caribbean. Winter sun, sea, and miles of golden sand.'

Lyle began to argue, but she put a finger to his lips.

'It's a holiday for you, Lyle,' she told him. 'You're right: you caught the tankard, so this holiday is your treat. I booked a special package for you. You'll have the time of your life.'

Lyle broke into a grin. 'You gorgeous thing!' he exclaimed as he hugged her. 'You're a real doll!'

'But I knew you wouldn't want to spend the time just lying on a beach.' Rachel gave him a knowing smile. 'That's why I booked you something that will suit you better... Two weeks on a boat, going deep sea fishing.'

Handbagged

Lara glanced at the clock and let out a muffled shriek. She was going to miss her train...

As she snatched up her old handbag, the strap broke. It had been frayed for a while, and was ready to go at any time – but why now? With a groan of frustration, Lara grabbed her purse and keys, and ran.

Passing the charity shop on the way to the station, she noticed an overflowing box of donations propped against the door. Someone had left it there overnight. It was full of old clothes. On top of the pile lay a handbag – a sleek, black, leather handbag, smarter than any Lara had ever owned.

Nobody was looking, so she picked up the handbag and hurried on her way.

She'd give some money to the charity shop another time.

She just managed to catch the train. Flopping down on a seat, she opened the handbag to put her purse and keys in there. She couldn't see a label. Yet surely, she thought, it must be a designer bag; it was so stylish – even more expensive–looking than she'd realised at first. Real class.

As she walked from the station to her office, she noticed women giving her envious glances. The bag seemed to whisper wealth. With it on her arm, Lara held her head high.

In the office, Barbara's eyes widened. 'Wow. That's a gorgeous bag! Where did you get it?'

'Online,' said Lara. 'It's nearly new.' In fact, it looked completely new. She wondered fleetingly why somebody would give it away.

It was such a lovely thing. Perhaps it had been an unwanted gift.

That reminded her: she needed to buy a present for her sister's birthday. So at lunchtime, she headed out with the handbag on her arm, and went to the smartest department store in town.

However, trudging round its glossy floors, Lara remembered why she so seldom came in here. She could barely afford anything on display. It was a shame, because Joanne would love that classy red purse set amidst the others on the counter...

Lara reached out to touch it. And before she knew it, the purse was in her handbag.

She was horrified. Why on earth had she done that? The assistant turned round to face her, so that now she couldn't replace the purse without being seen.

Lara could think of only one thing to do. With a thumping heart, she walked straight to the exit. As she stepped outside, she heaved a sigh of relief – until a stern voice behind her said, 'Excuse me. Could you accompany me to the office, please?'

A security guard stood there. Dumb with misery, Lara was led back into the building.

In a small, bleak room, a manager eyed her severely and told her to put her handbag on the table. How stupid am I, she thought wretchedly, visualising herself in court.

The security guard opened the sleek black handbag and took out her shabby brown purse and keys. Then he peered into the bag, checked the pockets, and held it upside down and shook it. Nothing fell out.

'I – I could have sworn...' he stuttered in confusion.

The manager studied Lara, who had come out shopping without her coat. She plainly had nowhere to hide a large red purse.

'There seems to have been some sort of mix-up,' he began apologetically.

Lara smiled coolly, like someone who could afford any number of fabulous handbags and had absolutely no need to shoplift.

'There certainly has,' she said. But she was bewildered. What had happened? There must be a hole in the bag's lining. When it was handed back to her, she was tempted to check at once.

But of course she couldn't look until she was outside again, well away from the shop. Then, on a quiet street corner, she opened the bag – and the first thing she saw was the red purse.

'What?' she said. The bag's lining was intact; where the purse had hidden itself was a mystery.

'Well, I can't take the purse back to the shop now, after all that! Anyway, Joanne will like it,' she decided.

On second thoughts, she reflected, maybe she would keep the red purse for herself. Why not? It was very elegant – much more in keeping with her smart new handbag than her tatty old purse was. She would buy Joanne a plant instead.

It occurred to Lara now that the handbag seemed too empty. Yet she shuddered at the thought of putting her cheap make-up and comb in that beautiful interior – to say nothing of her ancient phone.

It was time she had some new make-up. So, next day, Lara went shopping again.

This time she headed for the cosmetics section at the chemist's.

'Perfect!' she breathed, admiring an expensive lipstick. She was about to take it over to the till – when somehow her handbag fell open, and somehow the lipstick fell in.

'Bother. How did that happen?' But when Lara tried to fish it out, she couldn't see it in the bag. When she put her hand in, she couldn't even feel it. The lipstick was gone.

Puzzled, Lara left the store without buying anything – only to discover the lipstick inside the handbag on opening it two minutes later.

She stared into the bag's silky interior.

Maybe there's a secret compartment, she thought, bemused. However, if there was, she couldn't find it.

After some thought, Lara decided on an experiment.

She went into a different shop, where – without her trying – some costly eyeliner ended up inside her handbag. Once there, it disappeared till Lara was safely out of the door. Only then did it reappear in the bag.

She walked back to work as if in a dream, clasping the handbag tight. Its polished leather felt so wonderful, so smooth; but it was definitely still too empty. And so easy to fill...

So, the next day, the lipstick and eyeliner were followed by a pretty compact, and an expensive perfume. The day after that, she acquired some ear-rings and a rather lovely watch. Next was a designer diary with a pen to match. Then came an enamelled hairbrush and an elegant silver mirror.

Lara did not think too hard about these acquisitions. After all, it was the handbag that was doing this, not her. With it on her arm, she was drawn towards the most expensive and exclusive items on display. The handbag needed nice things; it deserved them.

As she walked back to the office after each trip, the handbag swinging on her arm, she felt wealthy, superior and invulnerable.

Nonetheless, once the bag was safely in her desk drawer, she began to feel pangs of guilt.

'That's enough,' she told herself as she settled back to work. 'I shouldn't be doing this. No more shopping tomorrow!'

So on Friday, Lara avoided the shops. She went to the nearby park to eat a sandwich. The place was sunny and crowded, but she squeezed onto a bench.

Next to her a girl was talking into the very latest, most expensive phone. On ending her call, she put it down on the bench beside her while she drank her coffee.

A moment later, she began to hunt around. 'Where's my phone? Have you seen my phone?' She checked anxiously under the seat.

'Oh dear,' said Lara sympathetically, jumping up to check the bench herself. 'I can't see a phone anywhere. Would you like to borrow mine?'

She opened the handbag wide enough to make it obvious that there was no phone in there, apart from Lara's old one. Taking this out, Lara offered it to her.

The girl shook her head, her eyes filling with tears as she scanned the passing crowds in suspicion and dismay.

Lara felt no compunction. If people didn't look after their nice things, they didn't deserve to keep them. As she strolled back to the office, she stroked the bag's perfect surface, before opening it to admire her shiny new phone.

She had lots of gorgeous things now to fill the bag with. That night she hid the whole lot in her wardrobe.

With the handbag out of sight, however, she lay awake, wondering what on earth she had been doing. Had she really taken all those things? She couldn't even use the phone without its pass-code! She had switched it off in something like horror.

Yet she still put it in her handbag the next morning. The handbag seemed to demand it. Looking in the mirror with the glossy bag on her arm, Lara felt dowdy. The bag needed smarter clothes to match it.

And it seemed the most natural thing in the world to acquire them.

So Lara visited the designer outlet. She soon discovered that the handbag was more capacious than it looked: it could happily hold a fine top or a cashmere scarf.

A security guard stopped her just as she was leaving with a silk blouse. Lara opened her handbag with lofty assurance, knowing that there would be no sign of the stolen garment. The guard's face was a picture of confusion when he peered into the empty bag.

This time she got a voucher as well as an apology. The blouse reappeared in her handbag ten minutes later: she wore it to work next day.

'What a lovely blouse,' said Barbara wistfully.

'Isn't it? I got it in a sale.'

'It's beautiful. By the way, Lara, I'm collecting for my heart charity,' said Barbara. 'Would you like to contribute?'

Lara cursed inwardly. That was the downside of wearing expensive clothes: people assumed you had money to throw away.

'Sure,' she said, reaching for the handbag. Then she frowned. 'Bother. I must have left my purse at home.' She had stopped using her old brown purse, preferring the new red one: but now, when she emptied the bag onto her desk, no purse at all appeared. 'Oh, well,' she said, with a shrug. 'Another time.'

Yet five minutes after Barbara had walked away, Lara checked her bag again. There was the purse.

Where had it been? This handbag seemed to have a mind of its own.

Well, now she could go and find Barbara to give her some money... but why bother? Why did she owe a heart charity anything? That sleek handbag had nothing to do with charity. Charity was for poor people. So Lara stayed where she was.

That evening, she met up with her sister Joanne for a birthday meal.

'Oh, lovely,' said Joanne doubtfully when she was presented with her cactus. 'How are you, Lara? You seem – different.'

'Different? How?'

Her sister looked uncertain. 'Well – smarter, I guess.'

'New make-up,' explained Lara.

'I like your top, and those gorgeous ear-rings. And that's quite a bag. Is it designer?'

'No,' said Lara shortly, and changed the subject.

She didn't enjoy chatting to Joanne as much as usual. Normally they had a giggle together; but today Lara kept noticing how cheap her sister's jewellery looked – and as for that shoddy polyester blouse!

Lara was glad when the meal ended. She paid reluctantly, since she had promised long ago that this would be her treat; but she didn't leave a tip. The staff hadn't been nearly respectful enough.

As they parted, Joanne said, 'Lara? Is everything all right?'

'Of course it is. Why do you ask?'

'Well, you just don't seem to be quite yourself today. I wondered if perhaps you were worried about something.

If there's anything wrong, you can always tell me, you know.'

Lara shrugged. 'There's nothing to tell.'

But her sister's words came back to her that night as she got ready for bed. She had left the bag downstairs. With it out of sight, she seemed to think more clearly. And she did not like her thoughts.

What on earth would Joanne say if she knew? Her sister – a shop-lifter and a thief! Lara saw herself afresh, and was appalled. What on earth had she been doing, letting herself be carried away by a fancy handbag?

'I won't do it any more,' she vowed. 'No more taking stuff that doesn't belong to me! I don't even need half of it. I know, tomorrow I'll take some of it down to the charity shop.'

So on Saturday, she went to the charity shop with a scarf and some jewellery in her hand.

'Oh, those are brilliant!' said the manageress when she handed them over. 'Thank you!'

It was only when she was about to leave that Lara realised that people in the shop were staring oddly at her. She looked down, to discover half a jumper hanging out of her smart handbag.

Lara stammered an excuse and put it on the rail. How on earth had it got there? It must have caught on the bag's buckle. Now everyone would think she was stealing from a charity shop! She had a hunch that she only got away unchallenged because of her donation.

And as she left the shop she had an even stronger feeling that – ridiculous though it seemed – the bag was angry with her.

It tried to pull her into a gift shop on the way home. Lara's foot was on the threshold before she managed to drag herself away. Forcing herself to walk past the jewellers' was even harder.

And the expensive shoe shop was a nightmare: her feet seemed to be stuck to the pavement. Getting away felt like wading through treacle. No, the handbag definitely did not want her to walk on.

Lara came to a decision. As soon as she got home, she emptied the handbag on to the kitchen counter.

Then she found her old bag with the broken strap, and set to work to mend it. Her mind was made up. She had to give up the new handbag. Maybe she should take it back to the charity shop – though she winced at the idea of showing her face there again.

She would stop using the bag, at least. Tomorrow she would go to work without it. After testing the mended strap, she tipped all her possessions into the old bag with determination.

Yet, when morning came, she dithered. Could she really bear to leave the wonderful new bag behind? It sat enticingly on the kitchen counter, waiting for her. It wouldn't take a minute to move her things back into it.

Lara wanted it so much. Or **it** wanted **her**...

She glanced at the clock, and screamed quietly.

Late again! There was no time to swap handbags. Snatching up her ancient, mended bag, she ran.

She just caught the train – but today it was standing room only.

Moving further down the carriage in a vain search for a seat, Lara recognised a face. It was the girl from the bench whose phone she had taken.

Lara slid through the packed bodies to reach her. The girl didn't look her way; and in the crush, she didn't feel anything as Lara slipped the phone into her coat pocket.

Leaving the train, Lara felt a wave of relief. That was one thing put right... but she wouldn't stop at returning the phone. She couldn't do anything about the used make-up, but she could give the red purse to Joanne after all – and find another charity shop for the clothes.

As soon as she arrived at work, she sought out Barbara to give her a donation.

Then, during her lunch break, she wandered through the shopping centre.

With her old bag on her arm, she dropped coins into every collecting box she saw. At each coin that fell, her heart seemed to lift.

On returning home that evening, Lara felt better than she had for weeks.

Until her house came into sight, and she saw the kitchen window...

The top pane of glass had been smashed so that the window could be forced open. She had left the handbag on the worktop, in full view: someone must have seen it and have been unable to resist.

Just like me, she thought. Now only shards of glass littered the worktop. The bag had gone.

Lara gazed around the kitchen, before checking the rest of the house. Nothing else seemed to have been taken.

She let out a long breath of relief and picked up her old phone. But on the point of ringing the police, she paused.

What would she tell them? How could she explain that the only thing stolen was an empty handbag?

And did she really want the handbag back? Lara changed her mind. She sat down in the kitchen, and rang a different number.

'Joanne? Hi, it's me. Sorry I was so off-hand last week. You were right, things weren't too good just then. I'll tell you all about it next time we meet up – can we make that soon? I'd really love to see you. Anyway, I'm much happier now...'

* * *

*

Printed in Great Britain
by Amazon

40352269R00092